D0563762

Fin-tastic Fashion

BY JESSICA YOUNG
ILLUSTRATED BY JESSICA SECHERET

PICTURE WINDOW BOOKS
a capstone imprint

Finley Flowers is published by Picture Window Books,
A Capstone Imprint
1710 Roe Crest Drive
North Mankato, Minnesota 56003
www.mycapstone.com

Library of Congress Cataloging-in-Publication Data is available
on the Library of Congress website.

ISBN: 978-1-4795-9804-5 (hardcover)
ISBN: 978-1-4795-9808-3 (paper over board)
ISBN: 978-1-4795-9828-1 (reflowable epub)
ISBN: 978-1-4795-9824-3 (eBook PDF)

Summary: Inspired by her sister Evie's favorite show, Finley decides to become a fashion designer. But just as Fin-tastic Fashions is taking off, Finley's mom finds out that Finley has been using the family's forks in the name of fashion. Finley has to wrack her brain to come up with another necessary accessory.

Editor: Alison Deering
Designer: Lori Bye

Vector Images: Shutterstock ©

Printed and bound in the USA.
010400F17

For Ingrid, and for Wes and Clara,
my designers and sporklet testers

TABLE OF CONTENTS

Chapter 1

DESIGN TIME

Finley had been counting the days till Saturday all week. She loved going on playdates at her friend Olivia's house. There was a huge playroom full of games and craft stuff, a tree house with a zip line, a zoo's worth of pets, and tons of great hiding places for hide-and-seek.

Unfortunately today Olivia wanted to play fashion show. Finley didn't have anything against fashion. She just had way more fun feeding Olivia's chinchilla, making up new recipes using her fancy kitchen gadgets, or skateboarding on her family's tennis courts.

"What do you think?" Olivia asked, spinning around in a floral dress.

"I like the way it flares out like a bell when you twirl," Finley said.

"It's definitely twirly," Olivia agreed. "Maybe I'll wear it with this sweater. The yarn has tiny gold flecks that sparkle in the light." She held the fabric up. "See?"

Finley nodded. "Sparkly."

"Check out this bracelet," Olivia said, pulling a small, velvet-covered box out of her desk. She took off the lid. "My Aunt Ingrid had it made just for me."

Finley peered inside, expecting something sparkly. Olivia loved sparkle. Instead, she saw a piece of smooth silver that was curled into a C resting on a bed of white satin. It was simple and bold — and different than anything Finley had ever seen.

"Wow." Finley ran a finger over the curved metal. "It's like a sculpture you can wear."

"Here," Olivia said. "Try it on."

Finley slipped the bracelet over her hand and onto her wrist. It felt smooth and cool, and it fit

perfectly. It was more than a piece of jewelry; it was a piece of art.

As she held it up admiringly, Finley got an awful feeling — like she was thirsty, and the only drink in the whole world was that bracelet.

"I like it," she said, quickly taking it off and handing it back. "It's different."

"It's one of a kind," Olivia said. "I don't know when I'll wear it. Maybe for a special occasion."

If it were mine, Finley thought, *I'd wear it every day.*

"It's really cool," she said as Olivia put it away.

"Thanks." Olivia searched through the mountain of clothes on her bed. Finally she pulled out a pair of purple cowboy boots. "What do you think of *these*?"

* * *

After Olivia finished with her fashion show, the two friends went outside. But the whole time they were playing trampoline circus, Finley couldn't focus.

Finley cheered for Olivia as she did a split jump and spun around in the air, but her mind was still stuck on something smooth and shiny. She remembered the previous summer, when her older brother, Zack, had been acting extra strange. Mom had said he had a crush on a girl and couldn't stop thinking about her.

Great, she thought as she watched Olivia bounce. *I have a crush on Olivia's bracelet.*

* * *

When Finley got home, Dad was working on the computer, and Evie, Finley's little sister, was watching TV. Evie wasn't choosy about what she watched — cartoons, game shows, commercials.

Sometimes Finley thought she might not be able to tell the difference.

Today Evie was watching *Design Time*. On this episode fashion designers raced against the clock to come up with fall-themed outfits. A man and woman were frantically cutting, pinning, and sewing. A model stood beside them, draped in fabric and looking bored.

"Sew faster!" Evie coached. "No, no — not a pink bow!" She shook her head. "They're never going to get done in time."

The camera zoomed out to show the rest of the studio. A long banner that read *Make a Fashion Statement!* hung from the ceiling. Across the room, another team of designers was outfitting a different model with thigh-high boots and a neon vest.

"Wow." Finley sat down next to Evie and took a swig of apple juice. "Nothing says *fall* like a reflective orange vest. She looks like a crossing guard."

Evie got her thinking-hard face. "Have you ever noticed that none of the designers dress in fancy clothes? They all just wear old T-shirts and ripped jeans."

Finley shrugged. "If the other choice was that orange vest, I'd pick a plain old T-shirt any day."

"I guess it's kind of like they have a free fashion pass," Evie said, picking the chocolate chips out of a bag of trail mix. "They're stylish no matter what."

Finley nodded. "Fashion designers don't have to worry about being in style — they *make* style."

She watched the designers flitting around the studio. Suddenly, she felt a Fin-tastic idea seed sprouting in her mind.

Maybe I could be a fashion designer! Finley thought. *Then I could make style too. After all, fashion is art, and I love art!*

She ran upstairs and got out her sketchbook. It was design time!

Chapter 2

SOMETHING FAD-ULOUS

Finley spent the rest of the afternoon scribbling in her notebook. She sketched a pair of pants with nineteen pockets — perfect for carrying her art supplies — then moved on to a jacket studded with jeweled constellations that reminded her of the night sky and a flouncy skirt made of fluttery fabric leaves.

When that was finished, she got down to brainstorming names for her new fashion brand. Finally, she settled on Fin-tastic Fashions. She liked the way it sounded. And the double F's made for a Fin-teresting logo.

Now all I have to do is decide on my first Fin-tastic fashion product, she thought, flipping through her sketches. *Something so noticeably new, so incredibly irresistible, that everyone will want one.*

Suddenly, a picture of Olivia's bracelet popped into Finley's mind.

Maybe I can make my own bracelet! she thought. *I'll use Olivia's for Fin-spiration.*

Finley turned to a clean page in her sketchbook. As she drew, she focused on what she liked about Olivia's bracelet. *It was smooth. Shiny. Simple. Silver . . .*

Finley drew and drew. Her pencil scratched across her page, leaving a trail of swooping, swirly curves. Before she knew it, she'd filled five pages of her sketchbook with bracelets. She paused and looked them over.

Too thick. Too thin. Too plain. Too fancy. Too curvy. Too straight. She turned to the last page. *What about that one?*

Finley ran a finger over the small sketch in the top corner. Then she held it up next to her wrist. Perfect.

Just then Mom padded into the living room with her coffee. "You've been busy," she said. "What are you working on?"

"I'm going to be a fashion designer," Finley told her. "I'm designing my first product."

Mom looked surprised. "Wow," she said. "I didn't know you had a passion for fashion."

"Me neither," Finley said. "But Evie's show made me realize that fashion is wearable art. It's a way to express yourself. That's why they call having your own style 'making a fashion statement.'"

"*I'm* making a fashion statement," Mom said, striking a pose in her T-shirt and sweatpants. "I'm saying, 'I am a woman who likes comfortable clothes!'"

Finley laughed. "But you're also saying, 'I like yellow.'"

"Not really," Mom said. "That's just the color that happened to be on sale."

* * *

At dinner, Finley glanced around the table at her family's outfits. *If I'm going to be a fashion designer,* she thought, *I need to think like one. I need to pay attention to what people wear.*

Dad was wearing what he wore most days: a plain, plaid shirt with buttons up the front. Zack had just finished a soccer game, so he was wearing his uniform. Evie had on a cropped, black sweater and the tattered tutu she'd used for her zombie ballerina Halloween costume. And Mom was still in her T-shirt and sweatpants.

"Can I ask you some questions?" Finley said, taking out her sketchbook. "I'm doing some research for my fashion line."

Zack smirked. "Fashion line?"

Mom shot him a knock-it-off look across the table. "Of course," she said to Finley. "We'd be glad to help."

"Okay," Finley said. "First question — what's your favorite color?"

"Probably blue," Mom said, serving Evie some salad. "Or maybe rusty orange. Or forest green. Or silver."

"Red," Zack said. "Red is the best color. Period."

"Uh-uh," Evie mumbled through a mouthful of rice. "Black."

"Black isn't a color." Zack smiled smugly. "We learned that in science."

Evie stuck out her chin. "It is too — we learned that in art."

"I've always been partial to maroon," Dad said.

Sheesh, Finley thought, scribbling notes in her sketchbook. *This is going to be hard. How can I design something people will like when everyone likes different things?*

"All right," she said. "Next question — when you're shopping for clothes, what makes you choose one outfit over another?"

"The price," Dad said matter-of-factly.

Finley sighed. "What if both outfits cost the same?"

"I'd pick the most useful one," Mom said. "Otherwise, I'd never wear it. 'Form ever follows function.'"

Finley crinkled her brow. "What does that mean?"

"A famous architect, Louis Sullivan, wrote it," Mom said. "But I think it makes sense for fashion too. It means the design of something reflects its purpose. Like, you wouldn't design a swimsuit made out of tissue paper."

"Or rocks," Zack added.

"Or an umbrella out of netting," Dad said.

"Or underwear out of thumbtacks." Evie giggled.

Finley thought about the fashions she'd seen on the magazine covers at the grocery store.

"But form doesn't follow function *all* the time," she said. "Sometimes fashions are just interesting or fun or beautiful. Sometimes we don't care if they're useful. What about all the people who wear high-heeled shoes?"

"Maybe they want to be really tall and reach stuff that's way up high," Evie suggested. "That's useful."

“I think you’re right,” Mom said to Finley. “Maybe form and function work together. And sometimes people wear things just because everybody else does.”

Dad cleared his throat. “You know, when I was younger, I was pretty stylish.”

Zack snorted.

“I’m serious,” Dad said. “I was one of the first kids in my grade to have parachute pants. And I break-danced in them too.”

“I’d love to see a video of that!” Zack said, reaching for the salad dressing.

“I wish I’d kept my leg warmers and my jacket with the huge shoulder pads,” Mom said. “What a crazy fad that was!”

“That was a bad fad,” Dad said, grimacing.

“What’s a fad?” Finley asked.

“When a style suddenly gets really popular and everyone is wearing it,” Mom explained, “like bell bottoms in the sixties or platform shoes in the seventies."

That's what I'm going to make, Finley thought. *Something fad-ulous.*

Chapter 3

SECRET SAMPLE

The next morning, Finley couldn't wait to get started on her first bracelet. *I need to make a sample,* she thought. *That way customers can see what they're ordering. But first I need a studio.*

She pulled the extra blanket off the end of her bed and hung one end of it on the wall hooks beside her desk. Then she stretched the other end over the back of her chair to make a tent.

Finley slipped into her chair and glanced around. *Ta-daah! Instant studio.*

Just then Zack knocked on her door. "Mom said to tell you she baked some cinnamon rolls." He peered in at her new construction. "What is *that*?"

"My studio."

Zack raised his eyebrows. "Your studio is a blanket fort?"

"It's only temporary," Finley explained. "Until I get a loft downtown like the one Evie and I saw on *Design Time*."

The corners of Zack's mouth crept up. "Riiiight."

"If you don't mind, I'd better get to work," Finley told him. "I've got fashions to design."

"Good luck, fashionista," Zack said.

Finley took out her sketchbook and flipped to the page with her best bracelet sketch. *I've got my design,* she thought. *Now what can I use to make a sample?*

Digging through her craft box, Finley found some metallic pipe cleaners and a roll of duct tape. *Maybe that'll do the trick.* She grabbed three pipe cleaners, braided them together, and bent them around her wrist.

Finley studied her creation and sighed. It didn't look anything like Olivia's silver bracelet. It looked like braided pipe cleaners.

She grabbed the duct tape and wrapped a piece around and around the pipe cleaners. When she'd finished, she slipped the bracelet back on. It was smooth and silver, but it still looked like duct tape.

Rummaging through her art supplies, Finley spotted a crumpled-up ball of tinfoil. She carefully un-crumpled it, then rolled and squeezed it to make a tight tube. Next she bent it to form a *C* and slid it onto her wrist, but it wouldn't stay put.

Finley sighed, scooped up her art stuff, and dumped it back into her craft box. It was time to take a break.

She went downstairs, helped herself to a cinnamon roll, and flopped onto the couch. Mom and Zack were watching Mom's favorite home show, which challenged contestants to create furniture and decorations out of old household items and junk. On this episode, the team was "bringing new life to old utensils" by making them into a chandelier.

"I hope that thing doesn't fall," Zack said as the design team hung the humungous light fixture above a fancy dining room table. "There's nothing like being skewered by fifty antique forks while you're eating dinner."

As Finley stared at all of the shiny silver forks, her brain started to buzz. *If they can use old stuff to create new furniture, maybe I can do the same thing to create new fashions. We've got lots of old stuff. In fact, why make a fake silver bracelet when I can make a real one?*

Finley slipped away silently and tiptoed to the kitchen, leaving Mom and Zack discussing the dangers of do-it-yourself projects. Then she quietly opened a drawer and held a salad fork up to the light.

Just what I need, Finley thought. *A Fin-tastic fork!*

Sliding the drawer shut, she slipped the fork into her pocket and headed to her room. But when she got to the stairs, she paused. She felt bad about taking something without asking.

Peering into the office, she found Dad sitting at his desk, staring at his computer screen.

"Hey, Dad," she said.

"Mm-hmm," Dad said, his fingers tapping out a rhythm on the keyboard.

Finley put her hand into her pocket and felt the fork. "Can I use one of our forks?" she asked casually. "I'm making something."

Dad kept typing. *Tap, tappity, tap, tap . . .* "Suuure," he said, without looking up.

Finley waited to see if he had anything else to add, but he didn't. *That was too easy,* she thought. *I should have asked him for a pet llama or a trip to Iceland.*

Once she was safely in her room, Finley closed the door behind her and pulled the fork out of her pocket. Grabbing both ends, she tried to bend it, but it wouldn't cooperate.

It was time to get creative.

Finley slunk down the basement stairs and found a hammer and some safety glasses. Slipping the glasses on, she held the fork as tightly as she could and braced it against one of the basement steps. Then she hit it with the hammer.

The fork flew out of her hand and landed in a laundry basket.

She tried again. It flipped and cartwheeled across the floor.

That's it, Finley thought. *I need help.*

She picked up the phone and called her best friend, Henry. "I need your assistance on a top-secret project," she whispered when he answered. "I'm calling an emergency meeting."

"Okay," Henry whispered back. "Hang tight. I'll be over in fifteen minutes."

"No — wait! Why don't we meet at your house?"

"Come on over," Henry said. "I'll be waiting."

Chapter 4
NECESSARY ACCESSORY

Finley wolfed down a quick peanut butter and jelly sandwich, then poked her head back into the office. "I'm going to Henry's for a bit, okay?" she asked over Dad's shoulder.

"Okay," he said, glancing at his watch. "Just make sure you're home by dinner."

Finley grabbed her sketchbook and ran down the street to the Lins' house, the fork in her pocket thudding against her leg. When she got there, Henry was waiting by the garage.

"Come on in," he said, holding the door open. "We can meet in here."

Finley stepped inside, and Henry pulled over two stools. "What's up?" he asked. "We've never had an emergency meeting before."

Finley looked around — no one was listening. "I decided what I want to be when I grow up."

Henry grinned. "You're already going to be an inventor, an artist, and a famous French chef," he reminded her. "What's the latest?"

"A fashion designer!"

"Wow." Henry's eyebrows shot up. "That wasn't what I was expecting. But you'd be great at it. You put together an amazing supernova costume for Halloween — and you made my vampire Elvis costume *fang*-tastic by sparklifying the cape."

"Thanks," Finley said. "Fashion is wearable art. And I love art."

"True," Henry said. "But I don't get it. Why is this top secret?"

"The top-secret part is my first product," Finley whispered.

Henry leaned in closer. "Which is . . ."

"Promise you won't spill the beans?"

Henry nodded and crossed his heart. "Promise."

"Before I can tell you, you have to officially join the Fin-tastic Fashions team — that's my new fashion brand."

"Okay," Henry said. "How do I do that?"

"You have to recite the Fin-tastic Fashions *Pledge of Elegance*." Finley opened her sketchbook and set it on Henry's lap. "I came up with it while I was brainstorming logos."

Henry read the pledge out loud. *"The Pledge of Elegance. I pledge elegance to the fad of the united statement of fashion, and to the design on which it stands, one notion understood, un-disposable, with outfits and accessories for all."*

He looked at Finley. "What exactly does that mean?"

"I'm not sure. But I thought it sounded good." Finley stood up and shook Henry's hand. "Anyway, welcome to Fin-tastic Fashions!"

"Thanks," Henry said. "I feel more fashionable already."

"Want to help me make a sample of our first product?"

Henry nodded. "Sure!"

Finley pulled the fork out of her pocket. "Ta-daah!"

“What’s that for, a picnic?” Henry asked hopefully.

“No. We’re making a bangle!”

Henry’s eyes lit up. “Great! Can we make it toasted with cream cheese?”

Finley sighed. “Not a bagel, a bangle.”

“Oh, a *bangle*!” Henry said. “Wait — isn’t that a type of tiger?”

Finley shook her head. “That’s Bengal. A *bangle* is a bracelet.”

“Oh.” Henry looked disappointed. “Right.”

“It’s the first in my new collection of necessary accessories,” Finley explained. “You can wear it, then eat with it. We just have to figure out how to bend this fork.”

“No problem,” Henry said, pulling over a bright red toolbox.

Finley looked through the toolbox. "First, we'll need to hold it still," she said, pulling out a clamp.

"You can clamp it to my mom's workbench," Henry suggested.

Finley followed Henry and clamped the fork to the workbench. She gave it a good tug to make sure it didn't move. "Hammer, please," she said, holding out her hand.

Henry passed her the hammer and some safety glasses. "Okay," he said. "Bang us a bangle!"

Finley put the glasses on. Then she brought the hammer down on the fork. *Clang! Clang! Clang!*

Slowly, the metal began to yield. Finley unclamped it, turned it around, and banged the other end.

"Not too much," Henry warned, "or you won't be able to eat with it."

"Good point," Finley said.

When the fork had curled into a *C*, Finley slipped it onto her wrist.

"Ta-daaah! Now *that* is a fashion statement!" She held her head high. "It says, 'I'm elegant!' It says, 'I'm bold!' It says, 'I'm ready to dig into whatever life dishes out!'"

"To me it says, 'I'm hungry!'" Henry said, taking the bangle and pretending to scoop up some air. "I love it. But a bagel bangle — *that's* a bracelet you could really sink your teeth into."

Finley laughed. "I think it might be time for a snack."

Henry handed the bangle back. "Come on. I'll whip up a tasty treat, and you can try out your newest creation."

Finley followed Henry to the kitchen. "I wish we had some PB&J Pasta," she said. "That would really put our bangle to the test."

Henry groaned. He loved thinking up new recipes, but he wasn't a huge fan of the spicy PB&J Pasta Finley had made for the school cook-off. "I'll think of something," he said, rummaging through the fridge. "Salty or sweet?"

"I'm in a sweet kind of mood," Finley said.

"Then sweet it is." Henry plunked a bowl of cut-up strawberries and some cream cheese onto the counter. "Did you know strawberries are packed with vitamin C? They're also members of the rose family."

Finley laughed. Henry was always full of interesting information. "Thanks for the random strawberry facts. What are you going to make?"

Henry wiggled his eyebrows. "You'll have to wait and see. It's going to be *berry* yummy."

He arranged the strawberries on a plate so they looked like the petals of a blooming flower. Then he spread some cream cheese onto each one and drizzled them with honey.

"There," he said, sliding the plate toward Finley. "Strawberry Cream Cheese Surprises. Let's give that bangle a whirl!"

Finley slipped the bracelet off.

"Drum roll, please." Henry drummed on the edge of the table as Finley speared a strawberry with the forked end of her bracelet and ate it.

“It works!” Henry announced. “Ladies and gentlemen, behold the — what is that thing called?”

“I haven’t named it yet,” Finley said, happily scooping up another strawberry. “Mmm, those *are* berry good.”

“Behold the yet-to-be-named whatchamacallit!” Henry said.

Finley washed off the bangle. “Your turn,” she said, passing it to Henry.

Henry speared two strawberries at once. “Look how much it holds,” he said. “This thing is great!”

Finley laughed. “I knew you’d be a good tester.” She glanced at the clock. “Uh-oh. I have to get home.”

“Don’t forget your thingamajig,” Henry said, handing the bangle back. He ducked inside the garage and returned with a clamp. “You can borrow one of these in case you want to make another bangle.”

"Thanks," Finley said as they stepped outside. "For your help and for the Hen-sational snack."

"Any time," Henry said. "Thanks for inviting me to join the Fin-tastic Fashions team and letting me take our first product for a test drive. Soon everyone's going to be wearing them!"

I hope so, Finley thought. *This could be the start of something big.*

Chapter 5
THE NEXT BIG THING

When Finley got to school on Monday, she hung her jacket in her cubby and plunked her books down on her desk. Slipping into her seat, she adjusted the bangle on her wrist and took out her silent reading.

She was just getting to the good part of the story when she noticed Olivia looking in her direction. Finley followed Olivia's gaze to the bangle on her wrist. She couldn't tell what Olivia was thinking. Did she like the bracelet, or not?

I guess I'll find out soon enough, Finley thought. *When Olivia doesn't like something, she doesn't try to hide it.*

Just then Finley's teacher, Ms. Bird, walked to the front of the room, her skirt swishing and her arms full of books. "Good morning, class," she said. "Please clear your desks of everything except your homework and a pencil."

As Finley bent down to put her book under her chair, the bangle slid off her wrist. It rolled across the floor and settled at Olivia's feet. Before Finley could scramble over to get it, Ms. Bird rang the chime.

"Take your seats please, everyone," she said. "It's time to get started."

Finley sank back into her chair and watched Olivia as she plucked up the bracelet and stuffed it into her desk. Finley waved to get her friend's attention, but Olivia's eyes were fixed on Ms. Bird, who had started going over word problems on the board.

Taking out her math notebook, Finley tried to follow along, but her thoughts kept drifting to the bracelet. Finally, Ms. Bird put down her marker and erased the board. It was break time.

Olivia made a beeline for Finley's desk. "What is this?" she asked, holding up the bangle.

Good question, Finley thought, wracking her brain for a name. "It's a . . ."

Before she could come up with an answer, their friends Kate and Lia swooped in.

"Wow!" Kate snatched the bracelet out of Olivia's hand. "That's so cool!"

"That *is* cool!" said Lia. "What is it?"

"It's a . . . a . . . forklet!" Finley said, thinking fast.

"A *forklet*?" Olivia raised an eyebrow. "What's it for?"

"It's for wearing," Finley said. "Like this." She took the forklet and slipped it around Olivia's wrist. "If you get hungry, you can eat with it too."

"Where did you get it?" Olivia asked.

"I made it," Finley said. "I'm going to be a fashion designer. The forklet is the first product in my collection of necessary accessories."

Olivia inspected the bracelet. "I like it. It's simple, yet stylish. You could wear it with pretty much anything. And you'll always be ready for a picnic."

"You can borrow it if you want," Finley offered.

"Okay," Olivia said. "I'll be your model."

"I've never seen anything like that," Kate said as Olivia walked away.

"No one has," Finley said. "It's the next big thing."

* * *

After class, Finley met Olivia at her cubby.

"I never realized a fork could be so stylish," Olivia said, twirling it around her wrist. "Accessories can make or break an outfit, and this would go great with just about anything. I wish I'd brought spaghetti for lunch so I could really test it out."

Suddenly, her eyes lit up. “Hey, maybe I could take it home to use at dinner!”

“You can keep it,” Finley said. “I’ll just make another one.”

“Wow, thanks!”

“I want one!” Lia said over Olivia’s shoulder.

“Me too!” Kate pleaded, clasping her hands together. “Pretty-pretty-please . . .”

"Okay," Finley said. "I'll bring them to school tomorrow."

Wow, she thought. *I'm going to be busy. I already have orders for three forklets! Make that four — I should bring one for Henry too.*

* * *

As soon as the dismissal bell rang, Finley hurried home. She had forklets to make.

Mom was in the front yard mowing the lawn. Finley gave her a wave then burst through the front door and speed-walked to the kitchen. She pulled out the silverware drawer and stared at the forks nestled peacefully in their places.

Dad said it was okay to use one, she thought. *I'm sure a few more won't hurt. We don't need* that *many forks for a family of five. Besides, I can always buy more once I sell some forklets.*

Checking the clock, Finley figured she had half an hour. It would be at least that long before Mom was done mowing and Dad got home from work. That gave her enough time to get her first Fin-tastic Fashions order done.

Finley picked out two salad forks for Kate and Lia and a dinner fork for Henry. Then she grabbed the clamp Henry had lent her, tiptoed downstairs, and pulled the hammer out of the toolbox in the basement.

Taking a deep breath, she clamped a fork to the worktable in the corner and started banging out bangles.

Hold on tight, Finley thought. *This fad's about to take off.*

Chapter 6
COPYCAT

Before class the next morning, Finley met Henry, Kate, and Lia by the cubbies. “I made your forklets,” she announced, passing them out.

“Thanks!” Kate and Lia said together.

“I’ve got miles of style!” Henry said, slipping his on and making a fist. “I feel like a fashion superhero!”

Just then Olivia walked up. “Now we all match!” She held up her arm to show off her forklet. “We’re going to start a trend.”

"Go forth and model," Finley told them. "And in case anyone asks, forklets are a dollar."

"A dollar is pretty cheap," Olivia said. "Are you sure that's the right price?"

"I want them to be affordable," Finley said. "Plus, we're trying to start a fad. The more we sell, the better."

Finley and her friends filed into class. As they took their seats, Ms. Bird closed the classroom door and turned on the projector. A picture of a blue lake and rolling green hills came up on the board.

"Good morning, class," the teacher said. "Raise your hand if you've ever been looking at a beautiful scene like this, and noticed something like *this*?" She clicked the remote, and the picture zoomed in to show a plastic bottle lying on the grass.

Finley raised her hand. A bunch of other hands went up around the room.

"There are lots of ways to help the environment," Ms. Bird said. "Today we're going to talk about waste. What is waste?"

"Waste is stuff we throw out," Henry answered.

Ms. Bird nodded. "And we throw out a lot — about two-hundred fifty-four million tons of trash a year in the United States."

"Gross!" Olivia blurted out.

"A lot of it ends up in landfills," Ms. Bird continued. "Some of it ends up in our oceans and waterways." She pointed to the plastic bottle. "That piece of plastic will be around way longer than we will. Four hundred and fifty years, to be exact."

"Yikes!" Kate said. "We use those all the time."

Ms. Bird nodded. "You're not alone. People are used to throwing things away. We don't think about the consequences, because we don't see where the garbage ends up."

Finley frowned. Thinking about all of that trash made her feel sick.

"But there are things we can do to help," Ms. Bird continued. "What's something you could do to stop using disposable bottles?"

Henry raised his hand. "I always take a refillable water bottle with me instead."

Ms. Bird smiled. "That's a great example of one of the three Rs — reduce. Think of all the plastic bottles you *didn't* use by refilling the one you have. Reducing can be summed up in two words: use less. Tomorrow, we'll talk more about waste and learn about the other two Rs — reuse and recycle."

As soon as Ms. Bird had finished, Henry turned to Finley. "Your forklets are a great example of reducing waste. You can use them again and again instead of buying disposable ones."

"Wow," Finley said. "I never thought of it that way. I guess fashion can be earth-friendly too!"

* * *

When Finley got home that afternoon, she headed straight for the silverware drawer. Henry, Olivia, Kate, and Lia had done such a great job modeling the forklets that everyone was talking about them. By the end of the school day, Finley had taken ten orders.

My forklets are fad-ulous, Finley thought. *There's no stopping them now!*

But as she neared the kitchen, she froze.

"Remind me to ask the kids to check their lunch boxes and backpacks for utensils," Mom was saying. "If they keep disappearing, we'll be eating with our fingers."

Finley's stomach sank. *Uh-oh,* she thought. *Maybe we needed all of those forks after all.*

She suddenly wished she could put them back, snug in their drawer. But the forks were forklets now. And customers were waiting — she had ten more orders to fill.

* * *

Finley crossed her fingers as she sat down to dinner. *Please don't ask about the missing forks,* she thought. *Pleasepleaseplease.*

"So," Mom said, glancing around the table, "what did everyone do today?"

Finley took a big bite of burrito so she wouldn't have to talk.

Zack heaped some salsa onto his plate. "Not much."

Dad turned to Evie. "What did you learn? Anything fun?"

"We learned about graphs," Evie said. "And how plants grow. Did you know that some plants are carnivorous? They eat *bugs*! I want a Venus flytrap for my birthday."

As Evie reached across the table for the salt, Finley noticed something silver around her wrist. Evie saw Finley looking and pulled down her sleeve.

But it was too late. Mom had seen it too.

"Evie," Mom said, "what's that on your arm?"

"What?" Evie asked, looking guilty.

Mom raised an eyebrow. "That shiny piece of metal that looks a lot like one of our spoons."

"Oh, that," Evie said. "Just something I made. Zack helped me, so I made him one too."

Zack pulled up his sleeve to reveal a matching spoon. "It was hard to bend, but it works great," he said. "I ate my yogurt with it at lunch."

Finley felt her cheeks flame. She couldn't keep quiet. "Copycat!" she said to Evie. "That's a fake!"

"A fake what?" Dad asked. "And how on earth can you tell?"

"It's a necessary accessory, and *I* made it first!" Finley snapped. "I thought of it, and I created it. Forklets are my fad, Evie — not yours!"

Evie glared. "For your information, this is a *spoon*let, not a forklet. I saw your friends wearing forklets at school, and I wanted to make something of my own."

Mom turned to Finley. "So you're saying it was your idea to use our utensils to make these . . . things?"

Finley stared at her plate. Somehow Mom made it sound so bad. *Why am I always the one who gets in trouble?*

Mom sighed. "Why didn't you ask?"

"I did ask," Finley said. "Dad said it was okay."

Dad looked surprised. "I did?"

"You said I could use a fork," she reminded him. "And I thought a few more wouldn't hurt. You were working on the computer, remember?"

Dad frowned. "I guess I wasn't paying attention."

Mom gave Dad a look. "I guess it's time to buy some new silverware."

"I'll help," Finley offered. "It's my fault we need more."

"We'll talk about it later," Mom said. "But for now, no more forklets *or* spoonlets. Utensils are for eating, *not* for wearing."

Chapter 7

THE 3 RS

Finley caught up with Henry in the hall the next morning. "Well, that fashion fad was a Fin-tastic failure," she said, plunking her backpack down beside her cubby.

"What do you mean?" Henry asked. "We were just getting started."

"Mom and Dad weren't exactly happy about me using the forks," Finley said. "Dad didn't even remember me asking. I'm going to have to tell all of our customers their forklet orders are canceled and refund their money."

Henry frowned. "I'm sorry. But I'm sure everyone will understand."

"I feel bad," Finley said. "I should have asked if I could use more forks, but it looked like we had so many. And I was planning on paying them back after I made it big."

"They'll forgive you," Henry said. "And you can pay them back once you think of a new product and sell millions of them."

Finley mustered a smile. "Thanks. You always know what to say." She unzipped her backpack and took out her books. "To make things worse, Evie made spoonlets without telling me. She's such a copycat."

"Who could blame her?" Henry said. "She knows a good idea when she sees it." He hung up his jacket. "Come on. Let's go."

Finley followed Henry into the classroom. The desks had been pushed together into groups of three. A cardboard box full of trash sat in the middle of each group.

"What is all this stuff?" Henry asked, taking a seat next to Finley.

Olivia set her bag down and sat across from Henry. "Ew. It looks like junk to me."

Finley pulled a plastic bottle out of the box. "I wonder what it's for."

Just then Ms. Bird got up from her desk and walked to the front of the room. "Good morning, class!" she said.

"Good morning!" everyone echoed.

"Yesterday we talked about waste and one of the three Rs — reduce," Ms. Bird said. "Does anyone know what the other two Rs stand for?"

"I think one stands for reuse," Henry said.

"Right," Ms. Bird said. "What are some ways to reuse?"

"You can donate things instead of throwing them away," Finley said. "Then someone else can use them."

Ms. Bird nodded. "Excellent."

"You can also use things in a new way," Henry added. "Like the time Finley made chain mail armor out of those pull-tabs on the tops of cans."

"Great idea." Ms. Bird smiled. "What about the third R — recycling?"

"I think that's when they pick up waste and make it into new things in a factory," Kate said.

"That's right," Ms. Bird said. "Waste is collected, sorted, and turned into different products."

"Like what?" Will asked.

Ms. Bird grabbed the bottle from Finley's desk and held it up. "Plastic waste like this bottle is used to make new bottles, toys — even chairs."

"Cool!" Henry blurted out. "We might be sitting on some right now."

Ms. Bird smiled. "Your group challenge today is to make a list of all the ways you could *reuse* the objects in the box in front of you," she continued. "You have fifteen minutes to brainstorm. Ready, set, go!"

"Who wants to be the list-maker?" Olivia asked.

Henry grabbed a piece of paper, and Finley handed him a pencil. "That would be me," he said. "I love lists."

Finley sorted through the box. "We've got a plastic bottle, some plastic grocery bags, some tinfoil, a milk carton, an egg carton, a candy bar wrapper, a cereal box, and a pretzel bag."

Henry turned to Finley. "Time for some of your Flower Power. What's growing in your idea garden?"

"We could cut the top off that bottle and make a vase," Finley said. "Or some kind of light . . ."

"Like the glow-stick lanterns we made at Camp Acorn!" Olivia said.

Finley turned the bottle over. "The bottom sort of looks like a flower. You could punch a hole in the center, then stick a pipe cleaner through it for a stem."

"It could be a planter," Henry said.

"Or a purse," Finley said. "You could braid the plastic grocery bags together to make the strap."

"What about a piggy bank?" Olivia suggested.

"A bird feeder!" Finley exclaimed.

"Hold on!" Henry said. "I'm writing as fast as I can!"

In the middle of brainstorming, Finley looked up to see Principal Small walking through the door. Finley's stomach did a cartwheel. The principal sometimes dropped by to see what see what they were studying in class. It always made Finley nervous.

Principal Small made her way through the islands of desks and stopped at Henry's. "This group sure seems to have a lot of ideas," she said, reading over his shoulder. "Keep up the good work. I can't wait to see what else you come up with."

Just then Ms. Bird rang the chime. "Okay, class," she said. "That's all the time we have for now."

"Too bad," Finley said. "I know we have more ideas."

"We always have more ideas," Olivia said. "Don't worry, this is plenty."

Henry handed Finley the paper. "Twenty eight to be exact."

* * *

At recess, it was time to break the bad news. Finley informed everyone that the forklets were discontinued and gave their money back.

Sheesh, she thought. *The fashion industry is tough.*

As Finley was heading to class, a first-grade boy followed her inside. "Excuse me," he said. "I'd like to order a forklet."

"Sorry," Finley said, "that product is no longer available. Our supplier ran out of materials."

"What does that mean?" the boy asked, looking confused.

Finley sighed. "It means forklets are finished."

Chapter 8

THE BEST IDEA EVER

At lunch, Finley found a quiet spot alone in the corner of the cafeteria. She was opening her yogurt when Henry slid his lunch tray along her table.

"How's it going?" he asked, taking a seat across from her.

Finley frowned. "Not so great. It's hard telling customers to forget the forklets. Everyone wants them even more now that they're gone."

"I know," Henry said, opening his lunchbox. "One first grader even offered me five bucks for mine."

"You should have taken it," Finley said glumly.

"Not a chance. I love my forklet." Henry scooped up some pasta salad. "Sorry you got in trouble."

Just then, Evie walked by with her second-grade class. As she passed Finley she stuck her nose in the air.

"What's up with her?" Henry asked.

"She's mad because she can't make any more spoonlets," Finley said. "And because I said she copied me — which she did."

"Would some of my pudding make you feel better?" Henry asked. "I'll get you an extra spork."

"That's okay," Finley said. "I'm not in a chocolate mood. Besides, I don't want to waste a spork, especially after talking about the three Rs."

"I'll make sure to recycle it," Henry said. "Although it would be better to reuse it. They should get metal ones. Sporks are definitely the best utensil ever."

Suddenly, Finley's eyes lit up. "Oh!" she jumped up, still holding her yogurt. "Oh-oh-oh!"

"What's wrong?" Henry said, standing up too.

"Nothing's wrong." Finley beamed. "You're brilliant!"

Henry raised an eyebrow. "I am?"

Finley nodded. "You just gave me the best idea ever!"

"Well, out with it!" Henry said.

Finley leaned across the table. "What if we could get people to reuse the plastic sporks from the cafeteria?"

"That would be great," Henry said. "We'd probably save hundreds of wasted sporks a day."

"Maybe if sporks were a fashion statement," Finley said, "people wouldn't throw them away."

Henry waved his spork like a magic wand. "That just might work."

Olivia plunked her lunchbox down beside Finley. "Everyone's asking about forklets," she said. "Too bad we don't have any more."

Finley nodded. "Yeah, the whole forklet thing didn't go quite as planned. But I think I just came up with something even better."

"What could be better than a forklet?" Olivia asked.

Finley held out her hand, and Henry passed her his spork.

"A *spork*let!" She held it up and spoke into it like a microphone. "With the new sporklet, you can make a fashion statement *and* help the environment by reusing."

“Leave it to you to take a great idea and make it even greater,” Henry said, taking back his spork.

“We’ll turn disposable sporks into wearable art, and keep them out of the trash,” Finley said. “It’s fashion with a mission!”

“Fashion with a mission,” Olivia echoed. “I like it.”

* * *

After school, Henry walked home with Finley. Half an hour later, Olivia’s mom dropped her off with a bag of supplies. Once Olivia had recited the *Pledge of Elegance,* Finley started sketching a sporklet design.

“Unlike the forklet, the sporklet will come in lots of different colors and patterns,” she explained, “so there’s something for everyone. We’ll use duct tape to make a band, which will fasten around your wrist with Velcro. Customers can pick their favorite colors and patterns of duct tape and personalize the bands."

"Sounds stylish," Olivia said.

Finley dug around in her craft box. "We've got Velcro squares and different kinds of duct tape," she continued, setting the materials on the kitchen table. "Plaid, sparky blue, skulls, tie-dye, and palm trees."

Olivia reached into her bag. "I have some purple polka-dot tape and some leopard print," she said, pulling out two more rolls and adding them to the collection. "And I brought some sporks. Mom always keeps the extras from fast food restaurants."

"Great!" Finley handed the safety glasses to Olivia. "First, we need to break a spork — short enough to fit on your wrist but long enough to eat with."

Olivia held a spork in both hands and tried to break it. "Arrgh. What kind of plastic is this?"

"Give it a whack on the back of your chair," Henry suggested.

Gripping the spork at each end, Olivia held it high, then brought it down on the back of the chair. It broke in two with a *crack*!

"Perfect," she said, holding up the pieces.

"Now, let's see your wrist," Finley instructed.

Olivia held out her wrist, and Finley measured it with a piece of yarn.

"Don't forget to leave room for the Velcro," Henry reminded her. "We want to make sure our sporks don't fall off."

Finley wrapped the yarn around Olivia's wrist two times. Then she cut the yarn and handed it to Olivia.

"It'll look better if we wrap the band around twice," she explained, "and it'll stay on better too." She pointed to the rolls of tape. "Pick a color."

"Let me guess," Henry said to Olivia, "you're still in your purple phase."

"Purple isn't a phase," Olivia said, giving him a look. "It's a way of life." She turned to Finley. "I'll have purple polka dot, please."

Finley cut the duct tape and laid it on the table, making sure to keep the sticky side up. Olivia passed her the spork.

"Hmm," Finley said, resting it on Olivia's wrist. "If the end is pointed down, it could poke you. But if it's sideways, it could poke someone else."

"Try it the other way," Olivia said turning the spork around. "Like this."

"Good call." Finley placed the spork on the duct tape and folded the tape in half lengthwise, lining up the edges to form a band. Then she wrapped the band around Olivia's wrist. "Looks good to me," she said. "Now for the Velcro."

"Did you know George de Mestral, a Swiss engineer, invented Velcro after going for a hike with his dog?" Henry said. "He was inspired by a burr that was stuck on his clothes. When he put it under a microscope, he discovered it had tiny hooks all over it that made it stick."

"How do you remember these random facts?" Olivia asked.

Henry shrugged. "I guess they just stick in my head — like Velcro."

He passed Finley the Velcro squares. She positioned them on the ends of the band and pressed them together.

"Look at that!" Henry said as Olivia held out her arm. "We turned trash into treasure!"

Olivia grinned. "I love it!"

"These are definitely better than forklets," Henry said. "With sporklets you can eat soup and salad at the same time! Everyone's going to want one."

"One?" Olivia shook her head. "They'll want one in every color!"

"Time for a sporklet assembly line," Finley announced.

She arranged all of the supplies on the table, and the team got to work. By the time Olivia's mom came

to pick her up, they'd made a whole collection of sporklets: two plaid, three sparky blue, three skulls, four tie-dye, two tropical, two purple polka dot, and two leopard print.

"Not bad," Henry said, surveying their finished products.

"Which one do you want?" Finley asked, motioning to the selection.

Henry grabbed a plaid one. "I'll start with a classic."

Finley took one with a tie-dye pattern, and the three friends put their wrists together.

"Three cheers for sporklets and Fin-tastic Fashions!" Finley said. "I can't wait to introduce our newest product!"

Chapter 9

SPECIAL OFFER

The next morning before class, Finley met Olivia and Henry at their cubbies. "Did you remember?" she asked, pulling up her sleeve to show her sporklet.

"Of course," Henry said, taking off his jacket. "I even wore my plaid shirt to match."

"Mine goes perfectly with my outfit," Olivia said, holding her sporklet up next to her sweater. "You can't go wrong with purple."

Finley took out her sketchbook and flipped to a page covered in strips of colored duct tape. "I made a sample sheet so people can see what their options are. And the next page is for taking orders."

"All right," Henry said, holding up his sporkleted wrist. "Let's sell some sporklets!"

Finley had just taken her seat and pulled out her silent reading book when Kate came running over. "What's that?" she asked, pointing to Finley's arm.

"That," Henry said from behind her, "is the latest creation from Fin-tastic Fashions — the sporklet!"

"You can wear it as a fashion statement, then roll up the band and eat with it, like this." Olivia demonstrated, holding the rolled-up band like a handle. "When you're done, just put it back on." She wound it around her wrist. "Voilà!"

"With the new sporklet, you can help save the environment and make a bold fashion statement at the same time," Finley explained. "It's available in a variety of colors and patterns to suit your mood and wardrobe."

"Wow," Kate said. "What colors does it come in?"

By the time Finley had spread the sporklets out on her desk, Lia, Will, and Tyra had all come over to look too.

"I like the tie-dye," Will said.

"I want a blue one," Kate said.

"How much are they?" Lia asked.

"You'd think an amazing product like this would be really expensive," Henry said. "But we're offering these sporklets for the special price of . . ." He looked to Finley.

Finley looked back. She'd been so busy designing the sporklets, she hadn't thought about the price. "Fifty cents!" she blurted out.

"Fifty cents?" Olivia shook her head. "That'll barely cover the cost of our duct tape."

"It's a *very* special offer," Henry said quickly. "And at a price like this, they won't last long — so get yours today!"

"I want one," Lia said.

"Me too!" Kate squeezed in closer. "But I only have thirty-five cents."

"It's okay," Finley said. "You can pay me later."

Suddenly, everyone was jostling to pick a color. Finley looked at the clock. Class was about to start.

"Form a line! Form a line!" Henry said as Finley handed out sporklets.

Just then, Ms. Bird walked through the door. Everyone scrambled to their seats. Finley swept the rest of the sporklets into her backpack just in time.

* * *

By the end of recess Finley had sold sixteen sporklets and collected $7.85. "Not bad," she said,

dropping the change into the small pocket of her backpack and zipping it up. "Now we can buy more duct tape."

"Just wait till the rest of the school sees them," Henry said. "Every person who wears one is like a walking sporklet commercial. Get ready to hire an assistant."

As Finley and Henry headed down the hall, Tyra came running up. "I need a sparkly blue sporklet!" she said. "Do you have any left?"

"Just a sec." Finley dug around in her backpack. "I'll see what I've got."

"You'd better hurry up, or you'll be late," Henry warned as he ducked into the classroom. "I'm going to get a start on homework — I've got soccer after school."

Finley was handing Tyra the last blue sporklet when she heard a familiar voice.

"Finley Flowers?"

Finley looked up to see Principal Small looming over her.

"I'd like to have a word with you," the principal said. "Please follow me."

Chapter 10
BIG TROUBLE

Principal Small marched toward the office, and Finley trailed behind her, nervoulsy clutching her backpack.

The office! she thought. *That's it — I'm a goner.*

Clip! Clop! Clip! Clop! Principal Small's shoes echoed down the hall. Finley's heart was beating so fast, she was sure it was echoing too.

When they got to the office, Principal Small held the door open and motioned for Finley to take a seat.

Then she clip-clopped to the other side of her desk and settled into her chair.

"Tell me about this," the principal said, holding up one end of a sparkly blue sporklet and letting the band unfurl.

Finley opened her mouth, but all that came out was a squeak. "It's a s-s-sporklet," she stammered, pushing up her sleeve to show her own. "You can wear it, then eat with it."

She demonstrated, coiling up the band and pretending to scoop something up. "It helps the environment by reducing waste from plastic utensils."

Principal Small wound the sporklet around her wrist. "You made it?"

Finley nodded.

The principal leaned forward in her seat and folded her hands. "Have you been selling these . . . things . . . at school?"

Finley nodded again and shrunk down in her chair.

"That's very creative," Principal Small said. "But school is a place for learning. Not selling." She set the sporklet on her desk and pointed to a sign on the office door. "See that?"

Finley nodded.

"It says *no selling things at school.* Why do you think we have that rule?"

Finley thought about all of the kids who'd crowded around her desk to buy a sporklet. "So we can focus on our work?"

The principal nodded. "Exactly. And so the teachers can focus on their work too."

Finley's heart pounded. She had broken a school rule. A big one. One that had its own sign posted on the office door.

She was officially in *big* trouble.

"I'm sorry," Finley said. "I didn't know."

"Well, now you do. You did show a lot of enthusiasm," Principal Small continued, "and I appreciate that. You also got me thinking. We use a lot of disposable utensils in the cafeteria. I'd like to work on phasing them out and getting reusable silverware and cups."

"Wow," Finley said, sitting up in her chair. "That's great."

"School rules aside, another problem with selling sporklets is that some kids might feel left out if they don't have money to buy one." Principal Small met Finley's eyes. "Have you ever wanted something that someone else has?"

Just then, an image of Olivia's silver bracelet popped into Finley's brain. She never wanted to make anyone feel how she'd felt about that bracelet. Suddenly, her fashion fad didn't seem so Fin-tastic after all.

"I'm sorry," she said softly, staring at the sporklet on Principal Small's desk. "I didn't even think of that. I wasn't trying to leave kids out."

"I know," Principal Small said. "And I'd like to propose a deal. No more selling sporklets at school, with one exception — if you'd consider having a portion of the money go to the school, I'd like to purchase a sporklet for every student in the fourth grade."

Finley's eyes lit up. "Whoa. That's more than sixty kids!"

Principal Small smiled. "Sixty-seven, to be exact. I'd provide the sporks of course. If it's too many for you to make —"

"No!" Finley said quickly. "It's not too many."

"Well, take your time," Principal Small said. "And one more thing. I'd love for our sporklets to show some school spirit. Do you think you could find duct tape in our school colors?"

Finley grinned. "I know I can!"

Chapter 11

WHAT YOU CAN'T HAVE

After school, Finley went to Olivia's house. The two friends made seven sporklets, then sat on Olivia's bed and flipped through her magazines.

"Wow, look at that awesome loft!" Finley said, holding up a picture of a huge room with wide windows looking out on a busy city street. "I'd trade all my craft supplies for a studio like that."

"But then you wouldn't have any craft supplies, so you wouldn't be able to make anything," Olivia pointed out. "I get it, though. You always want what you can't have."

Finley turned to Olivia. "Have you ever felt that way?"

"Sure," Olivia said. "I've wanted *lots* of things I can't have."

"Really?" Finley said. "Like what?"

"Like a baby harp seal. And a tree fort with a glass bridge to my bedroom window. And your freckles . . ."

Finley's mouth dropped open in surprise. "I thought you didn't like freckles!" she exclaimed. "You tried to wipe mine off on the first day of kindergarten. You said you were 'cleaning' my face."

Olivia laughed. "Actually, that was the *second* day of kindergarten. On the *first* day of kindergarten I couldn't stop looking at them."

“That’s right!” Finley said. “I remember you staring at me.”

“I *loved* your freckles,” Olivia said. “After school, I went to my room and drew dots all over my face with marker so I could have some too. My mom was so mad. It took a lot of scrubbing to clean them off.”

Finley laughed and shook her head. "I can't believe you did that."

"The next day at school, I tried to wipe your freckles off," Olivia continued. "I figured if I couldn't have them, then you shouldn't either."

"Wow," Finley said. "I had no idea."

"Sorry," Olivia said. "I've always felt bad about that."

"Why didn't you tell me?"

Olivia shrugged. "It's kind of embarrassing. Plus, it was such a long time ago. I thought maybe you forgot."

"That's not the type of thing you forget," Finley said. "But I've got an idea for our next Fin-tastic Fashions product — stick-on freckles!"

"I like it!" Olivia said. "I would have paid big money for those."

"They could even come in different colors," Finley said. "Blue, orange . . ."

"Sparkly purple!"

Finley laughed. "Hey, thanks for telling me. If I could have shared my freckles, I would have."

Olivia smiled. "I know," she said. "You're a good friend."

* * *

"I'm going to have to find another place to sell my sporklets," Finley announced at dinner. "It's against the rules to sell stuff at school."

"Well, I'd like to order five sporklets," Mom said. "We'll keep them in the car for picnics or for when we go out to eat. Then we won't have to use disposable ones — and we'll look stylish too."

"Great!" Finley said. "You can place your order, but you might not get them for a while. Principal Small just ordered one for every fourth-grade student."

"What?" Zack said. His eyes grew wide. "That must be —"

"Sixty-seven sporklets." Finley finished for him. She grinned proudly and turned to Mom. "I'm donating some of the money to the school, and I'm going to use the rest to pay you back for the forks."

Mom smiled. "I appreciate the offer," she said. "But you should keep it. You can buy materials to make more sporklets."

Finley shook her head. "I have to pay you back somehow," she insisted. "If it weren't for me, you wouldn't have had to buy more silverware."

"All right," Mom said. "I'll make you a deal. How about giving me five free sporklets? We'll call it even."

"How about a lifetime supply of free sporklets?" Finley suggested.

Mom laughed. "Are you sure you want to offer that? I might want a set in every color."

Finley nodded. "I'm sure. I'll show you the color samples after dinner."

* * *

Once the dishes were done, Finley pulled out her sporklet samples to show Mom.

"I've been thinking," she said, "if I'm going to be a fashion designer, I'd like to get some more Fin-teresting clothes. I want to develop my own sense of style."

"If you want to be in style, you'd better plan on making a lot of money," Zack said.

"That's not true," Evie said. "You don't have to spend a lot of money to be fashionable. You can go treasure hunting at used clothing stores and put together some great outfits. I saw it on *Design Time*."

"You can also look for things you like and wait until they go on sale," Mom said. "I was thinking — you've outgrown a lot of your old clothes. Maybe you could have a yard sale."

"Great idea," Finley said. "Someone else might be happy to have them."

"I have some things to sell," Zack said, heading for his room.

"Me too!" Evie bolted upstairs.

Finley's eyes lit up. "Maybe I'll sell some sporklets!"

Chapter 12
YARD SALE

On Friday afternoon, Finley, Evie, and Zack made yard sale signs for Mom to post around the neighborhood. Then they hunted through their closets and drawers and labeled their yard sale items with color-coded price stickers.

"Orange is two dollars, yellow is one dollar, green is fifty cents, and blue is twenty-five cents," Evie said. "I'll write it down so we don't forget."

"What's red?" Zack asked.

"Red is expensive," Finley said. "It's for big-ticket items only — five dollars."

"I'd forgotten about some of this stuff," Zack said as he folded a button-down shirt and stuck an orange label on it.

"Me too," Evie said. "Look at this!" She held up a frilly dress that was way too small.

Finley laughed. "I think that used to be mine."

"Well, now someone else can enjoy it," Evie said. "I'm pretty sure you won't be needing it anymore."

When they'd finished labeling all of their items, Finley made a Fin-tastic Fashions sign and checked to make sure she had plenty of sporklets in every color.

* * *

The next morning, Finley, Evie, and Zack got up extra early. They stretched a piece of rope between two trees in the front yard to make a clothesline and hung up their old clothes on hangers.

Zack and Finley carried out two folding tables.

"I'll be the cashier," Zack said, setting the cash box full of change on one of the tables. "I'm good at managing money. In fact, I was thinking, as your company starts to grow, I could help with the business part."

Finley grinned. "I'll think about it." She draped a couple of old skirts over the other table and set up her Fin-tastic Fashions sign, fanning out her sporklets in front of it.

"We'd better hurry up," Evie said. "It's almost time to start the sale."

"I think I might have to learn to sew," Finley said, surveying the clothes as they swayed on their hangers. "Then I could take all of those outfits apart and put them back together in Fin-teresting ways."

Ard
Sale

"The sleeves from that sweater could be leg warmers," Evie suggested. "And you could use the strap from that purse as a belt."

"That's not a bad idea," Finley said.

Evie beamed. "Maybe I could help. We could call our company Flowers Fashions."

Finley smiled. "That has a nice ring to it." Even though Evie could be a copycat, she was still her little sister. Life was much better when they worked together.

Taking a seat behind her sporklet table, Finley took out her sketchbook so she could dream up some new designs. It fell open to her first page of bracelet sketches.

Finley studied them. The more she thought about it, it wasn't Olivia's bracelet she'd really wanted. Sure, it was shiny and special and different — but it was more the *idea* of it she'd been stuck on. Like somehow if it were hers, she'd be shiny and special and different too. And the fact that it was Olivia's had just made her want it more.

Like Olivia said, you always want what you can't have, Finley thought, playing with the sporklet on her wrist. *Strange how that works.*

"Did you make those?" a voice asked.

Finley looked up to see a young boy pointing to the sporklets on the table. He was about four or five, with dark eyes, long lashes, and a crown of thick, black curls.

Finley nodded. "I did."

"What are they?" he asked.

"They're sporklets. You can wear them — and eat with them."

The boy's eyes lit up as Finley demonstrated how the sporklet worked. "How much are they?" he asked, dumping a handful of pennies on the table. "I've got this much."

FIN-TASTIC
fASHiONS

It wasn't even close to fifty cents, but Finley didn't care. "That's how much they are," she said. "Which one do you want?"

The boy grinned and grabbed a tie-dye sporklet. Finley helped him wrap it securely around his wrist and fastened the Velcro.

"Thanks!" he said. Then he turned and ran back to where a man with a stroller waited on the sidewalk. "Dad! Dad! Look what I got!"

Just then Zack ambled over. "Wow," he said, pointing to the pile of pennies. "First sale of the day. You're going to be rich."

"Ha." Finley grinned and handed him a penny. Somehow it felt like she already was.

About the Author

Jessica Young grew up in Ontario, Canada. The same things make her happy now as when she was a kid: dancing, painting, music, digging in the dirt, picnics, reading, and writing. Like Finley Flowers, Jessica loves making stuff. When she was little, she wanted to be a tap-dancing flight attendant/veterinarian, but she's changed her mind! Jessica currently lives with her family in Nashville, Tennessee.

About the Illustrator

When Jessica Secheret was young, she had strange friends that were always with her: felt pens, colored pencils, brushes, and paint. After Jessica repainted all the walls in her house, her parents decided it was time for her to express her "talent" at an art school — the famous École Boulle in Paris. After several years at various architecture agencies, Jessica decided to give up squares, rulers, and compasses and dedicate her heart and soul to what she'd always loved — putting her own imagination on paper. Today, Jessica spends her time in her Paris studio, drawing for magazines and children's books in France and abroad.

Make Your Own Sporklet

Don't throw away that plastic spork! Create your own Necessary Accessory.

What You'll Need:

- plastic spork (preferably one you've already used at a restaurant or in the school cafeteria)
- patterned or colored duct tape
- scissors
- Velcro patches
- safety glasses

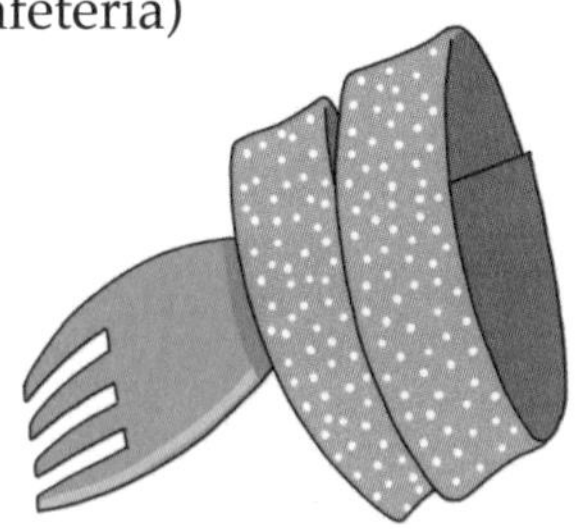

What to Do:

1. Put on your safety glasses and break off the spork about 1–1 ½ inches from the end you eat with. Try pressing it against a table edge or the back of a wooden chair to break it in the right spot — or ask an adult for help.

2. Measure your wrist using a cloth tape measure or a piece of string. Be sure to wrap it around your wrist twice when measuring so your sporklet band will be long enough to stay on.
3. Choose a color or pattern of duct tape for the sporklet band. Cut it to the measured length by placing the tape measure or string beside it before cutting.
4. Stretch the duct tape out (sticky side up) on a table or desk. Place the spork perpendicular to the tape so that about 1/2 inch (1.3 cm) of the handle overlaps the tape about one inch in from the end of the strip.
5. Carefully fold the tape lengthwise and press the sides together. (The end of the spork handle will be sandwiched between the two sides of the folded duct tape.)
6. Wrap the band around your wrist twice, then use a Velcro patch to secure it. Stick one side of the patch underneath the end of the band and stick the other side on the facing part of the band so it can fasten.
7. Make sure to wear your sporklet when you go out to eat so you can avoid using disposable utensils — and make a fashion statement!

Henry's Strawberry Cream Cheese Surprises

These yummy, bite-sized strawberry snacks are surprisingly easy to make. Ask an adult to cut the strawberries — and help you eat them!

What You'll Need:

- strawberries
- cream cheese
- honey

What to Do:

1. Wash the strawberries, and ask an adult to cut the tops off and cut them in half.
2. Spread a layer of cream cheese on each strawberry.
3. Put all of the strawberries on a plate and drizzle them with honey.

Be sure to check out all of Finley's creative, Fin-tastic adventures!

Finley Flowers
Super Spooktacular
by Jessica Young
Finley Flowers
by Jessica Young
New & Improved
Finley Flowers
Room to Bloom
by Jessica Young
Finley Flowers
Pet-Rified
by Jessica Young